Date: 7/8/14

J 741.5 WOL
David, Peter
Wolverine, first class. Hand in
hand, part 1 /

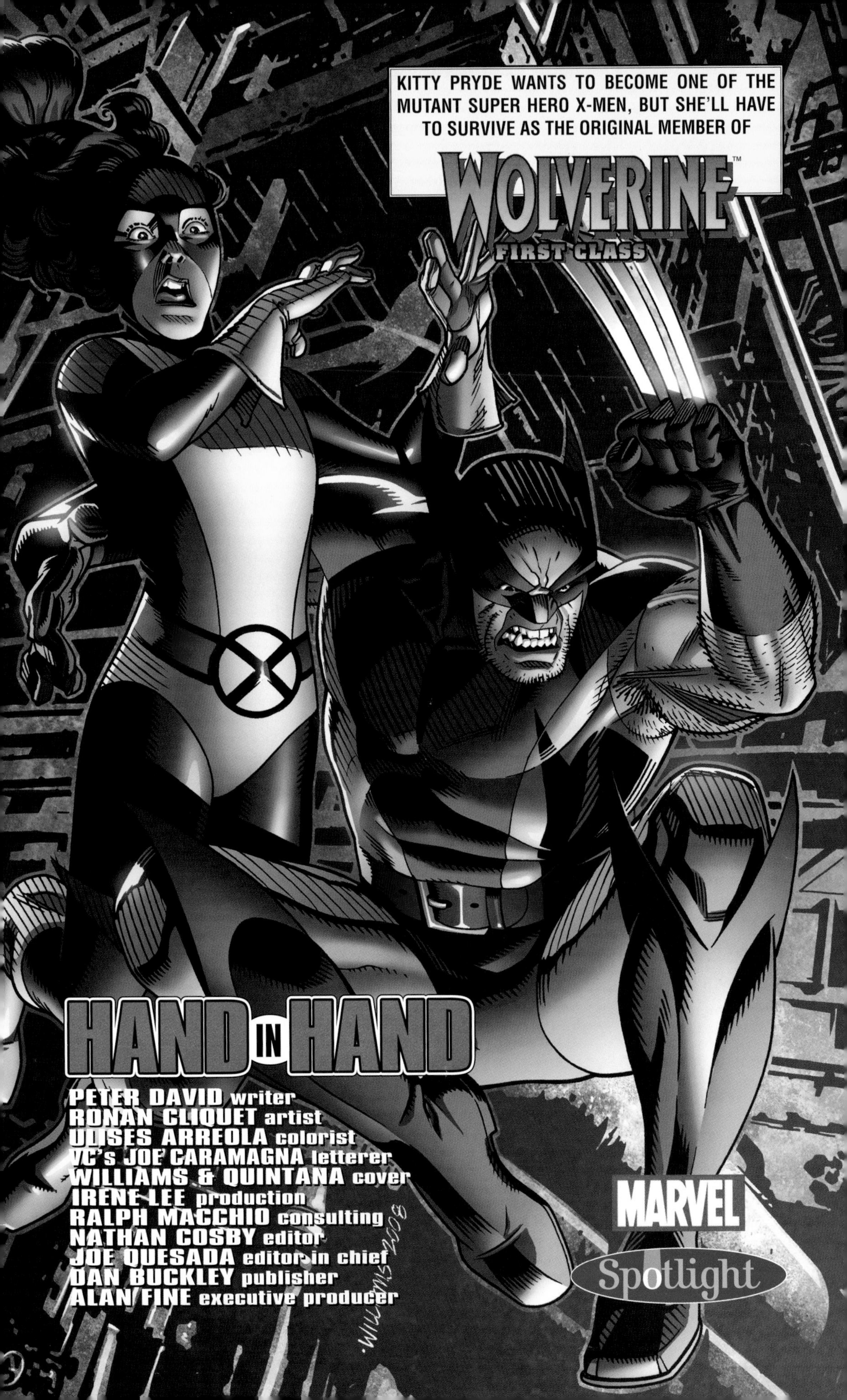
KITTY PRYDE WANTS TO BECOME ONE OF THE MUTANT SUPER HERO X-MEN, BUT SHE'LL HAVE TO SURVIVE AS THE ORIGINAL MEMBER OF
WOLVERINE™
FIRST CLASS
HAND IN HAND
PETER DAVID writer
RONAN CLIQUET artist
ULISES ARREOLA colorist
VC's JOE CARAMAGNA letterer
WILLIAMS & QUINTANA cover
IRENE LEE production
RALPH MACCHIO consulting
NATHAN COSBY editor
JOE QUESADA editor in chief
DAN BUCKLEY publisher
ALAN FINE executive producer
MARVEL
Spotlight

Visit us at www.abdopublishing.com

Reinforced library bound editions published in 2014 by Spotlight, a division of the ABDO Group, PO Box 398166, Minneapolis, MN 55439. Spotlight produces high-quality reinforced library bound editions for schools and libraries. Published by agreement with Marvel Characters, Inc.

Printed in the United States of America, North Mankato, Minnesota.
042013
092013
This book contains at least 10% recycled material.

Library of Congress Cataloging-in-Publication Data

David, Peter (Peter Allen)
[Graphic novels. Selections]
Hand in hand / story by Peter David ; art by Ronan Cliquet. -- Reinforced library bound edition.
volumes cm. -- (Wolverine, first class)
"Marvel."
Summary: "Kitty Pryde usually likes museums, but wouldn't you know it...the art gallery that Wolverine's taken her to is run by the evil Hand (they're Ninja types), which means that Daredevil & Elecktra can't be too far away from the action"--Provided by publisher.
ISBN 978-1-61479-176-8 (part 1) -- ISBN 978-1-61479-177-5 (part 2)
1. Graphic novels. [1. Graphic novels. 2. Superheroes--Fiction.] I. Cliquet, Ronan, illustrator. II. Title.
PZ7.7.D374Han 2013
741.5'352--dc23

2013005933

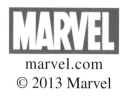

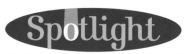

All Spotlight books are reinforced library bindings and manufactured in the United States of America.

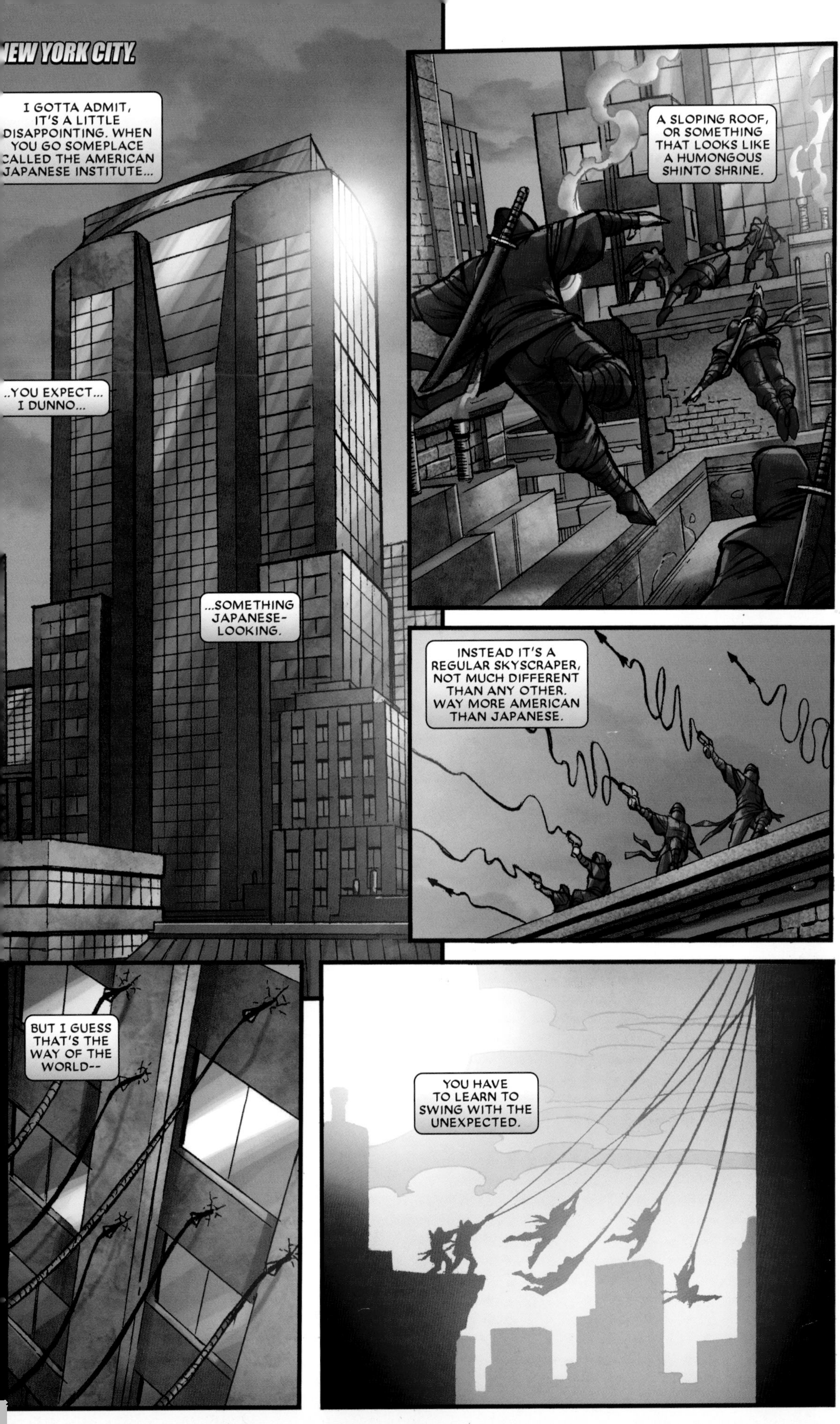
NEW YORK CITY.
I GOTTA ADMIT, IT'S A LITTLE DISAPPOINTING. WHEN YOU GO SOMEPLACE CALLED THE AMERICAN JAPANESE INSTITUTE...
..YOU EXPECT... I DUNNO...
...SOMETHING JAPANESE-LOOKING.
A SLOPING ROOF, OR SOMETHING THAT LOOKS LIKE A HUMONGOUS SHINTO SHRINE.
INSTEAD IT'S A REGULAR SKYSCRAPER, NOT MUCH DIFFERENT THAN ANY OTHER. WAY MORE AMERICAN THAN JAPANESE.
BUT I GUESS THAT'S THE WAY OF THE WORLD--
YOU HAVE TO LEARN TO SWING WITH THE UNEXPECTED.

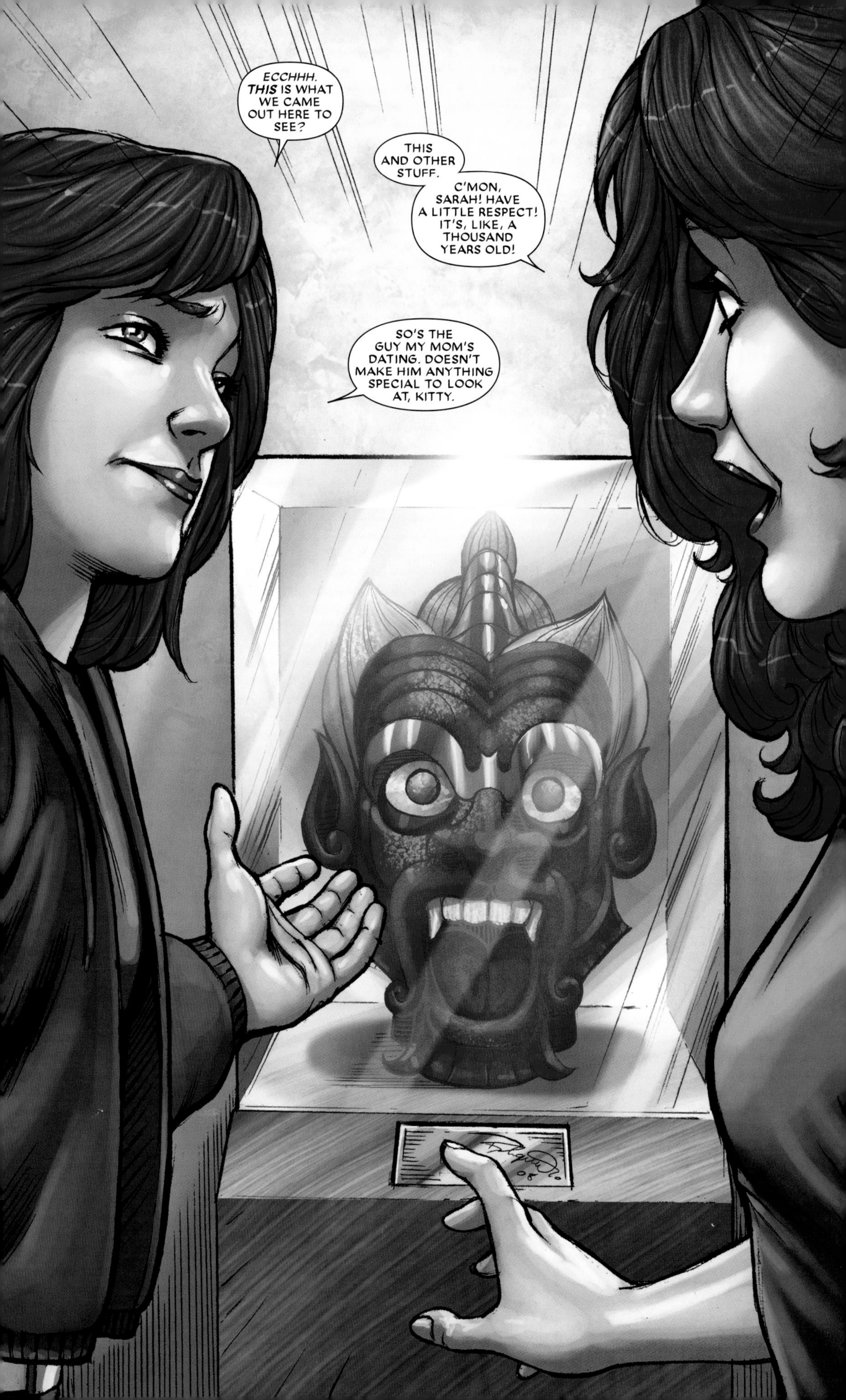
ECCHHH. THIS IS WHAT WE CAME OUT HERE TO SEE?
THIS AND OTHER STUFF.
C'MON, SARAH! HAVE A LITTLE RESPECT! IT'S, LIKE, A THOUSAND YEARS OLD!
SO'S THE GUY MY MOM'S DATING. DOESN'T MAKE HIM ANYTHING SPECIAL TO LOOK AT, KITTY.

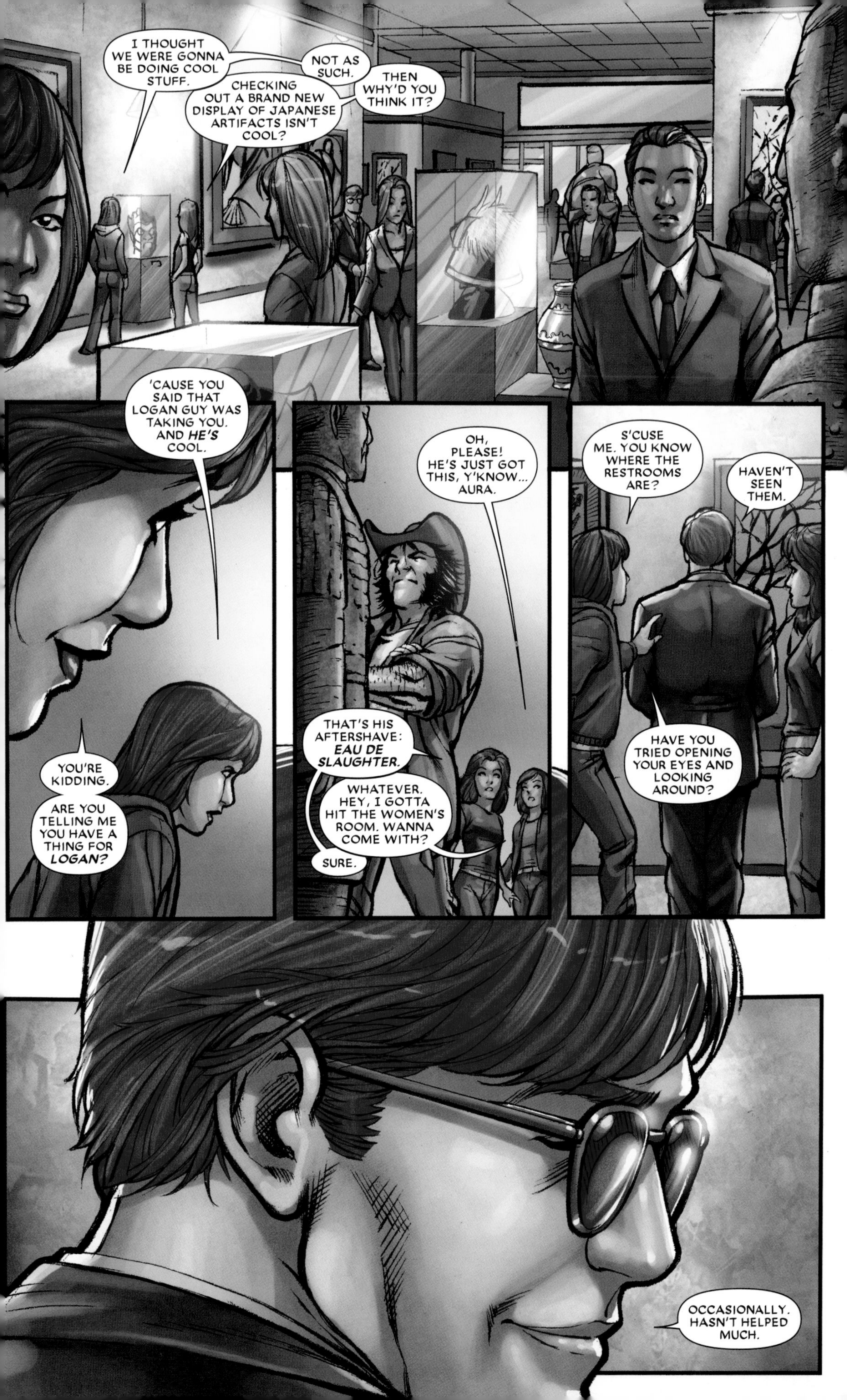
I THOUGHT WE WERE GONNA BE DOING COOL STUFF.
NOT AS SUCH.
CHECKING OUT A BRAND NEW DISPLAY OF JAPANESE ARTIFACTS ISN'T COOL?
THEN WHY'D YOU THINK IT?
'CAUSE YOU SAID THAT LOGAN GUY WAS TAKING YOU. AND HE'S COOL.
YOU'RE KIDDING.
ARE YOU TELLING ME YOU HAVE A THING FOR LOGAN?
OH, PLEASE! HE'S JUST GOT THIS, Y'KNOW... AURA.
THAT'S HIS AFTERSHAVE: EAU DE SLAUGHTER.
WHATEVER. HEY, I GOTTA HIT THE WOMEN'S ROOM. WANNA COME WITH?
SURE.
S'CUSE ME. YOU KNOW WHERE THE RESTROOMS ARE?
HAVEN'T SEEN THEM.
HAVE YOU TRIED OPENING YOUR EYES AND LOOKING AROUND?
OCCASIONALLY. HASN'T HELPED MUCH.

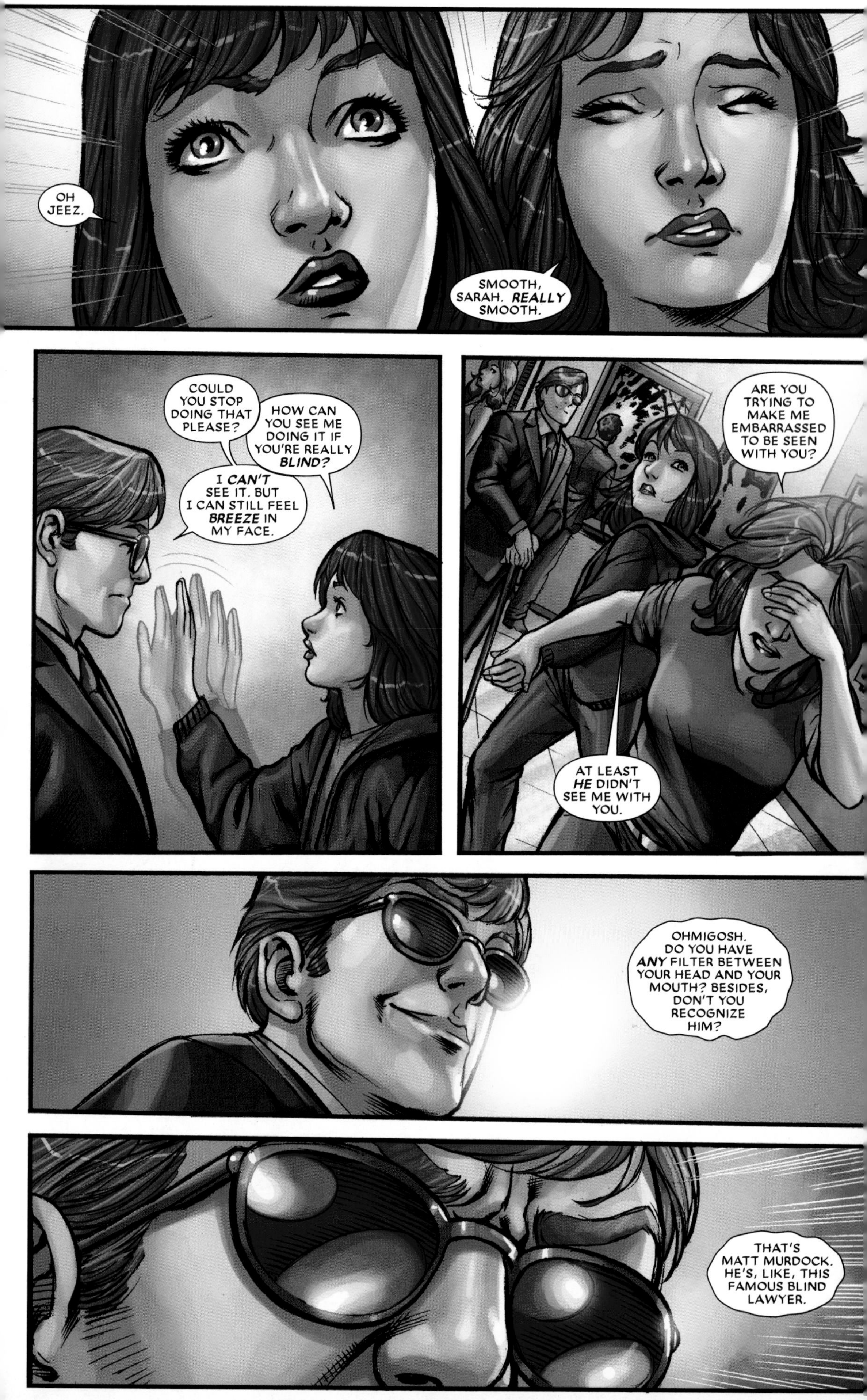
OH JEEZ.
SMOOTH, SARAH. REALLY SMOOTH.
COULD YOU STOP DOING THAT PLEASE?
HOW CAN YOU SEE ME DOING IT IF YOU'RE REALLY BLIND?
I CAN'T SEE IT. BUT I CAN STILL FEEL BREEZE IN MY FACE.
ARE YOU TRYING TO MAKE ME EMBARRASSED TO BE SEEN WITH YOU?
AT LEAST HE DIDN'T SEE ME WITH YOU.
OHMIGOSH. DO YOU HAVE ANY FILTER BETWEEN YOUR HEAD AND YOUR MOUTH? BESIDES, DON'T YOU RECOGNIZE HIM?
THAT'S MATT MURDOCK. HE'S, LIKE, THIS FAMOUS BLIND LAWYER.

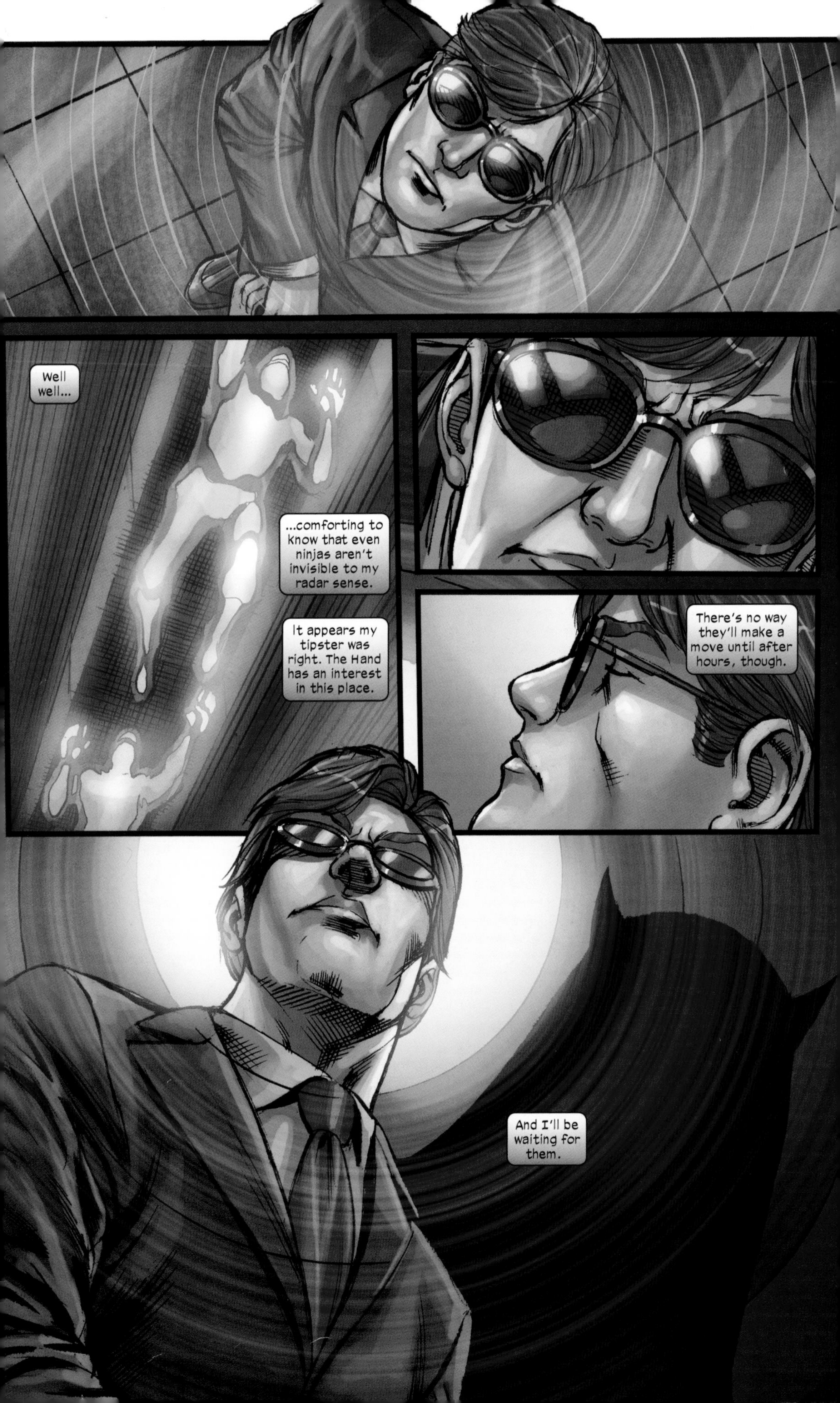
Well well...
...comforting to know that even ninjas aren't invisible to my radar sense.
It appears my tipster was right. The Hand has an interest in this place.
There's no way they'll make a move until after hours, though.
And I'll be waiting for them.

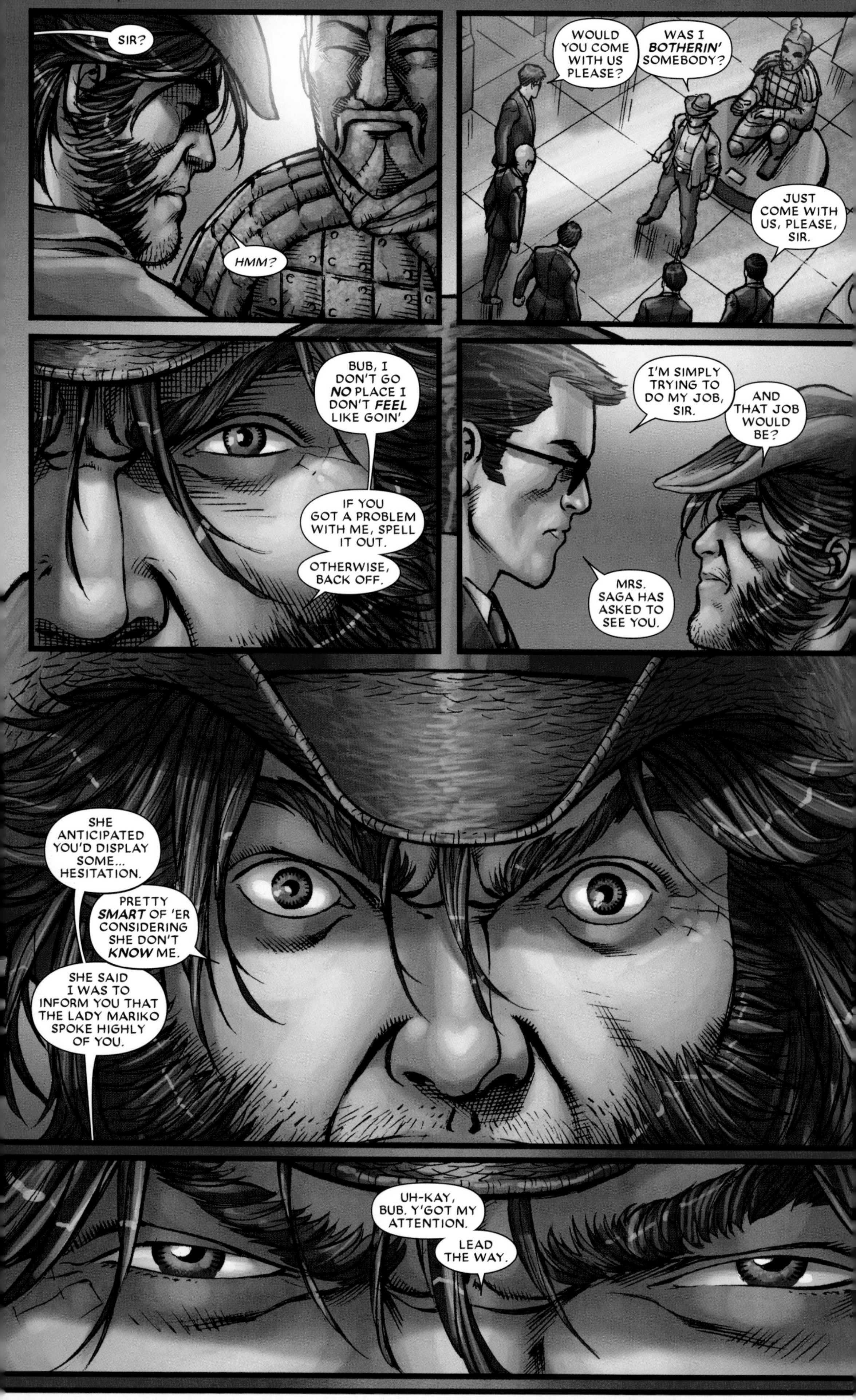
SIR?
HMM?
WOULD YOU COME WITH US PLEASE?
WAS I *BOTHERIN'* SOMEBODY?
JUST COME WITH US, PLEASE, SIR.
BUB, I DON'T GO *NO* PLACE I DON'T *FEEL* LIKE GOIN'.
IF YOU GOT A PROBLEM WITH ME, SPELL IT OUT.
OTHERWISE, BACK OFF.
I'M SIMPLY TRYING TO DO MY JOB, SIR.
AND THAT JOB WOULD BE?
MRS. SAGA HAS ASKED TO SEE YOU.
SHE ANTICIPATED YOU'D DISPLAY SOME... HESITATION.
PRETTY *SMART* OF 'ER CONSIDERING SHE DON'T *KNOW* ME.
SHE SAID I WAS TO INFORM YOU THAT THE LADY MARIKO SPOKE HIGHLY OF YOU.
UH-KAY, BUB. Y'GOT MY ATTENTION.
LEAD THE WAY.

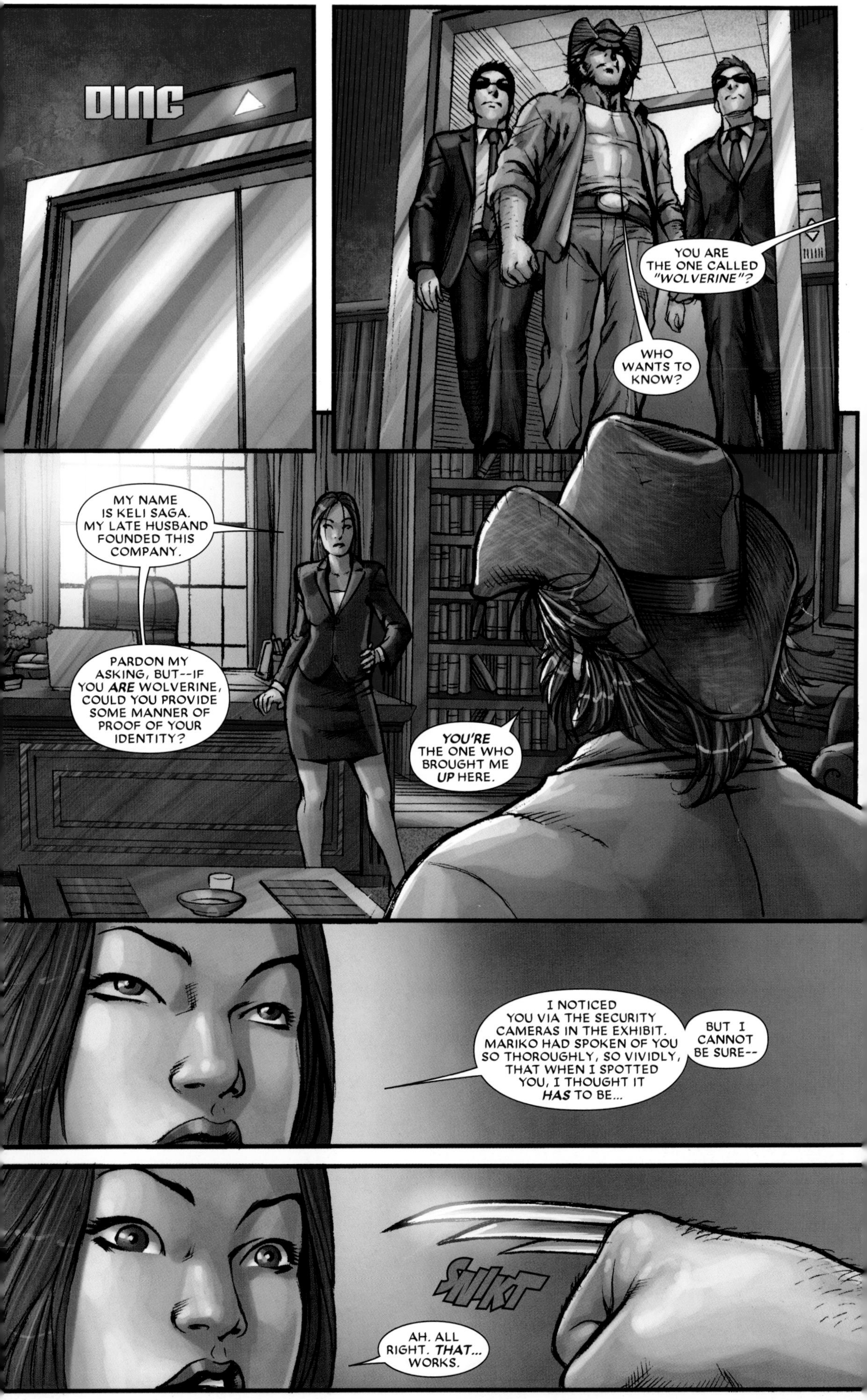
DING
YOU ARE THE ONE CALLED *"WOLVERINE"*?
WHO WANTS TO KNOW?
MY NAME IS KELI SAGA. MY LATE HUSBAND FOUNDED THIS COMPANY.
PARDON MY ASKING, BUT--IF YOU ***ARE*** WOLVERINE, COULD YOU PROVIDE SOME MANNER OF PROOF OF YOUR IDENTITY?
YOU'RE THE ONE WHO BROUGHT ME ***UP*** HERE.
I NOTICED YOU VIA THE SECURITY CAMERAS IN THE EXHIBIT. MARIKO HAD SPOKEN OF YOU SO THOROUGHLY, SO VIVIDLY, THAT WHEN I SPOTTED YOU, I THOUGHT IT ***HAS*** TO BE...
BUT I CANNOT BE SURE--
SNIKT
AH. ALL RIGHT. ***THAT...*** WORKS.

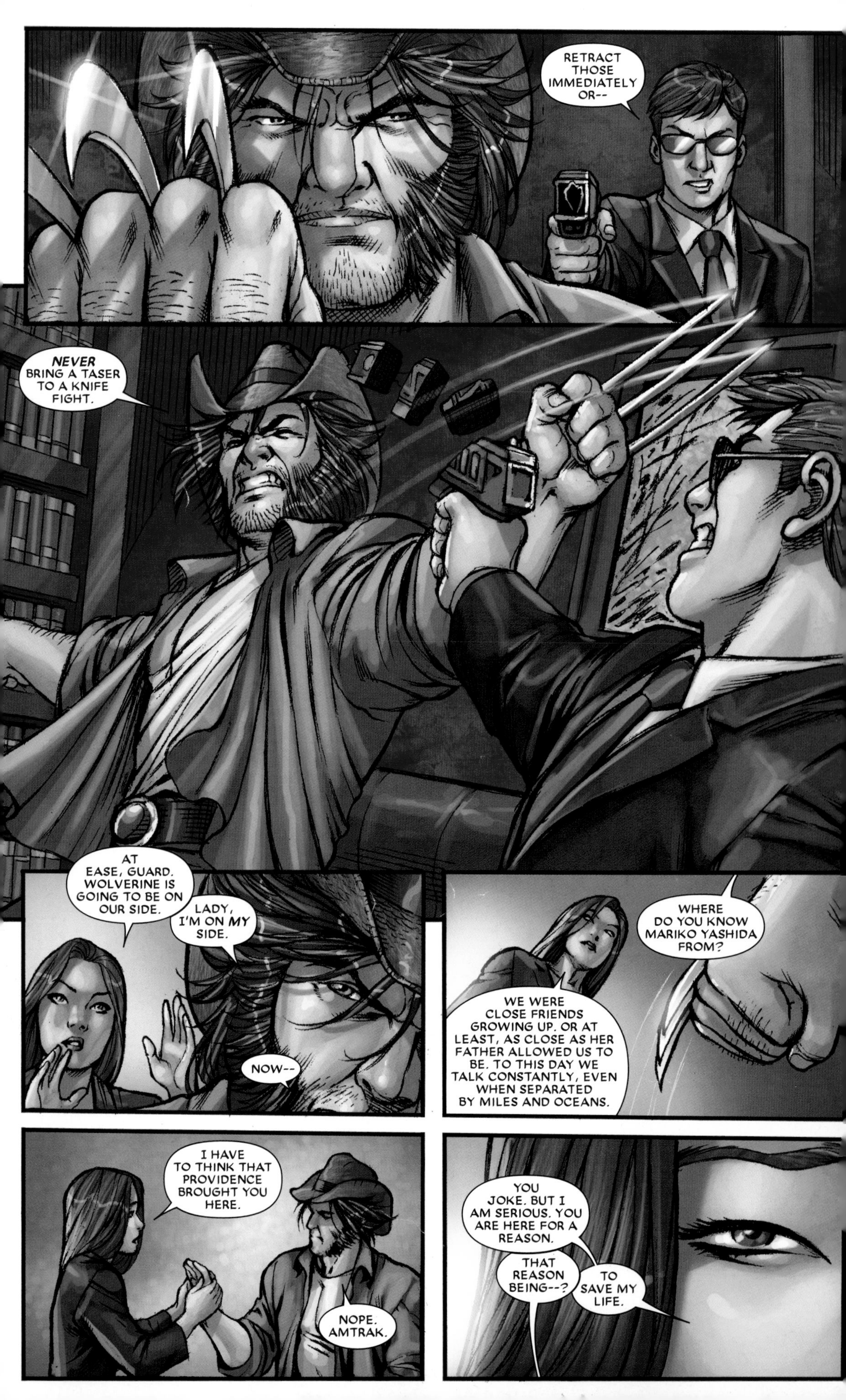

RETRACT THOSE IMMEDIATELY OR--
NEVER BRING A TASER TO A KNIFE FIGHT.
AT EASE, GUARD. WOLVERINE IS GOING TO BE ON OUR SIDE.
LADY, I'M ON MY SIDE.
NOW--
WHERE DO YOU KNOW MARIKO YASHIDA FROM?
WE WERE CLOSE FRIENDS GROWING UP. OR AT LEAST, AS CLOSE AS HER FATHER ALLOWED US TO BE. TO THIS DAY WE TALK CONSTANTLY, EVEN WHEN SEPARATED BY MILES AND OCEANS.
I HAVE TO THINK THAT PROVIDENCE BROUGHT YOU HERE.
NOPE. AMTRAK.
YOU JOKE. BUT I AM SERIOUS. YOU ARE HERE FOR A REASON.
THAT REASON BEING--?
TO SAVE MY LIFE.

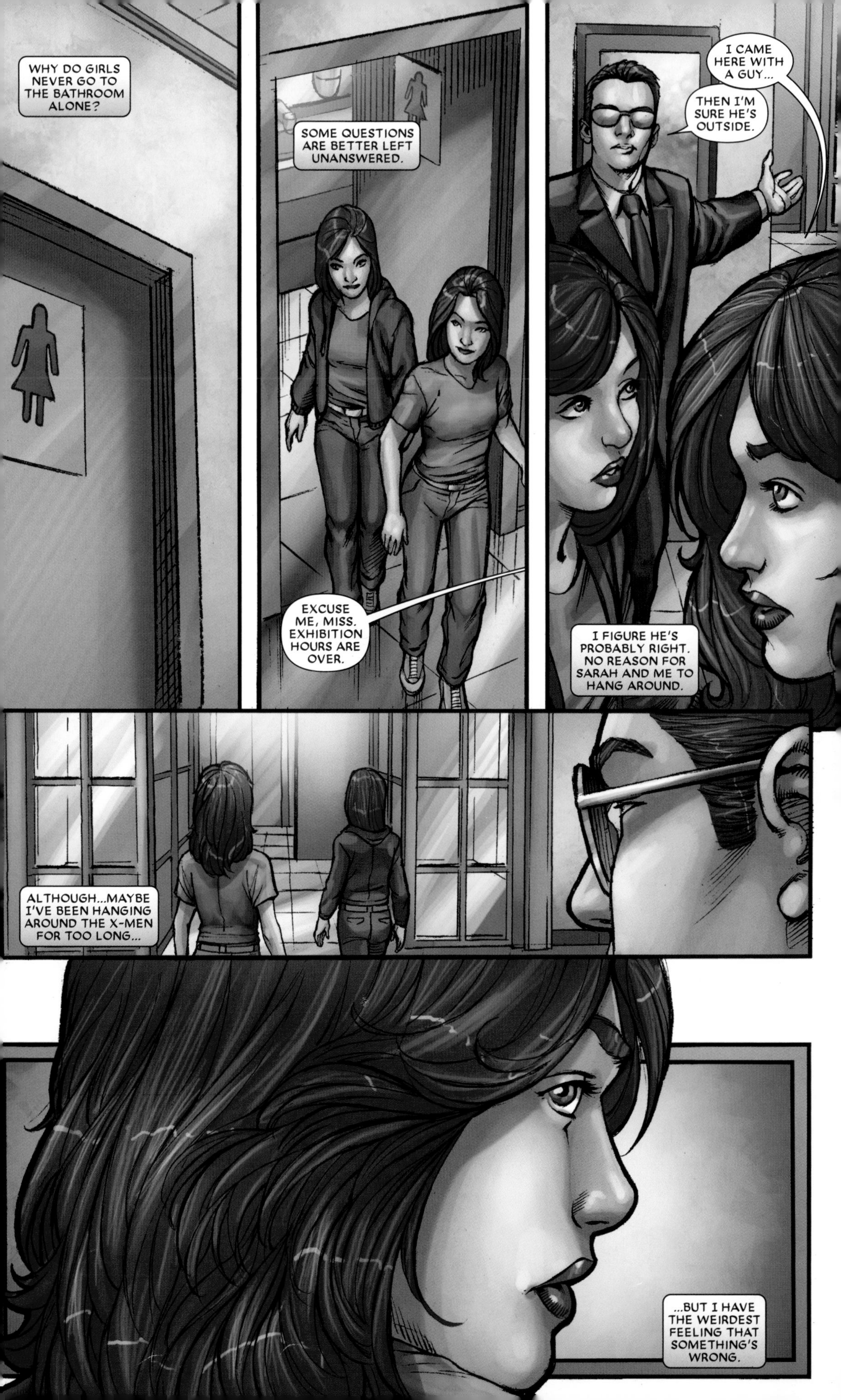
WHY DO GIRLS NEVER GO TO THE BATHROOM ALONE?
SOME QUESTIONS ARE BETTER LEFT UNANSWERED.
EXCUSE ME, MISS. EXHIBITION HOURS ARE OVER.
I CAME HERE WITH A GUY...
THEN I'M SURE HE'S OUTSIDE.
I FIGURE HE'S PROBABLY RIGHT. NO REASON FOR SARAH AND ME TO HANG AROUND.
ALTHOUGH...MAYBE I'VE BEEN HANGING AROUND THE X-MEN FOR TOO LONG...
...BUT I HAVE THE WEIRDEST FEELING THAT SOMETHING'S WRONG.

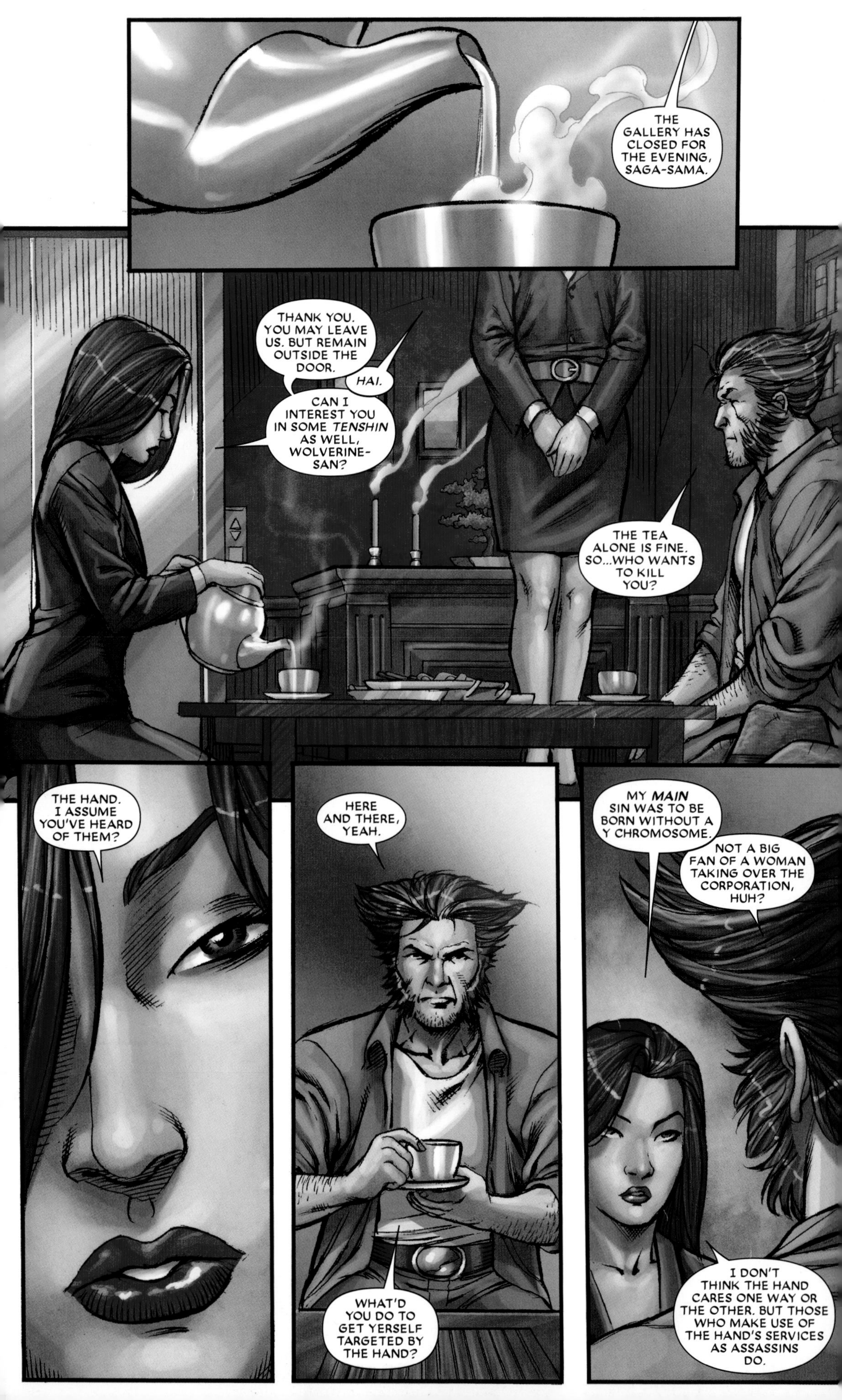
THE GALLERY HAS CLOSED FOR THE EVENING, SAGA-SAMA.
THANK YOU. YOU MAY LEAVE US. BUT REMAIN OUTSIDE THE DOOR.
HAI.
CAN I INTEREST YOU IN SOME TENSHIN AS WELL, WOLVERINE-SAN?
THE TEA ALONE IS FINE. SO...WHO WANTS TO KILL YOU?
THE HAND. I ASSUME YOU'VE HEARD OF THEM?
HERE AND THERE, YEAH.
WHAT'D YOU DO TO GET YERSELF TARGETED BY THE HAND?
MY MAIN SIN WAS TO BE BORN WITHOUT A Y CHROMOSOME.
NOT A BIG FAN OF A WOMAN TAKING OVER THE CORPORATION, HUH?
I DON'T THINK THE HAND CARES ONE WAY OR THE OTHER. BUT THOSE WHO MAKE USE OF THE HAND'S SERVICES AS ASSASSINS DO.

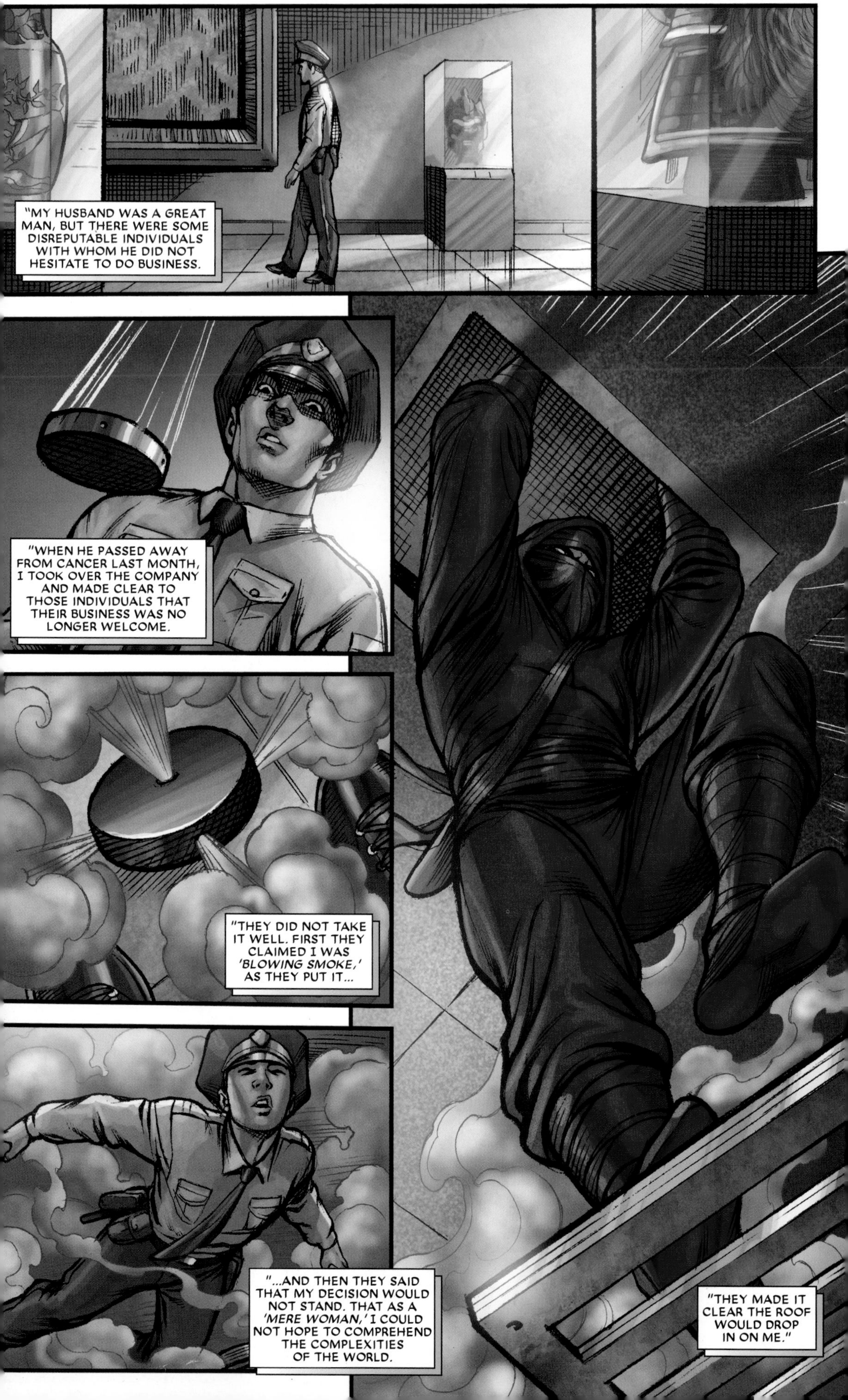
"MY HUSBAND WAS A GREAT MAN, BUT THERE WERE SOME DISREPUTABLE INDIVIDUALS WITH WHOM HE DID NOT HESITATE TO DO BUSINESS.
"WHEN HE PASSED AWAY FROM CANCER LAST MONTH, I TOOK OVER THE COMPANY AND MADE CLEAR TO THOSE INDIVIDUALS THAT THEIR BUSINESS WAS NO LONGER WELCOME.
"THEY DID NOT TAKE IT WELL. FIRST THEY CLAIMED I WAS *'BLOWING SMOKE,'* AS THEY PUT IT...
"...AND THEN THEY SAID THAT MY DECISION WOULD NOT STAND. THAT AS A *'MERE WOMAN,'* I COULD NOT HOPE TO COMPREHEND THE COMPLEXITIES OF THE WORLD.
"THEY MADE IT CLEAR THE ROOF WOULD DROP IN ON ME."

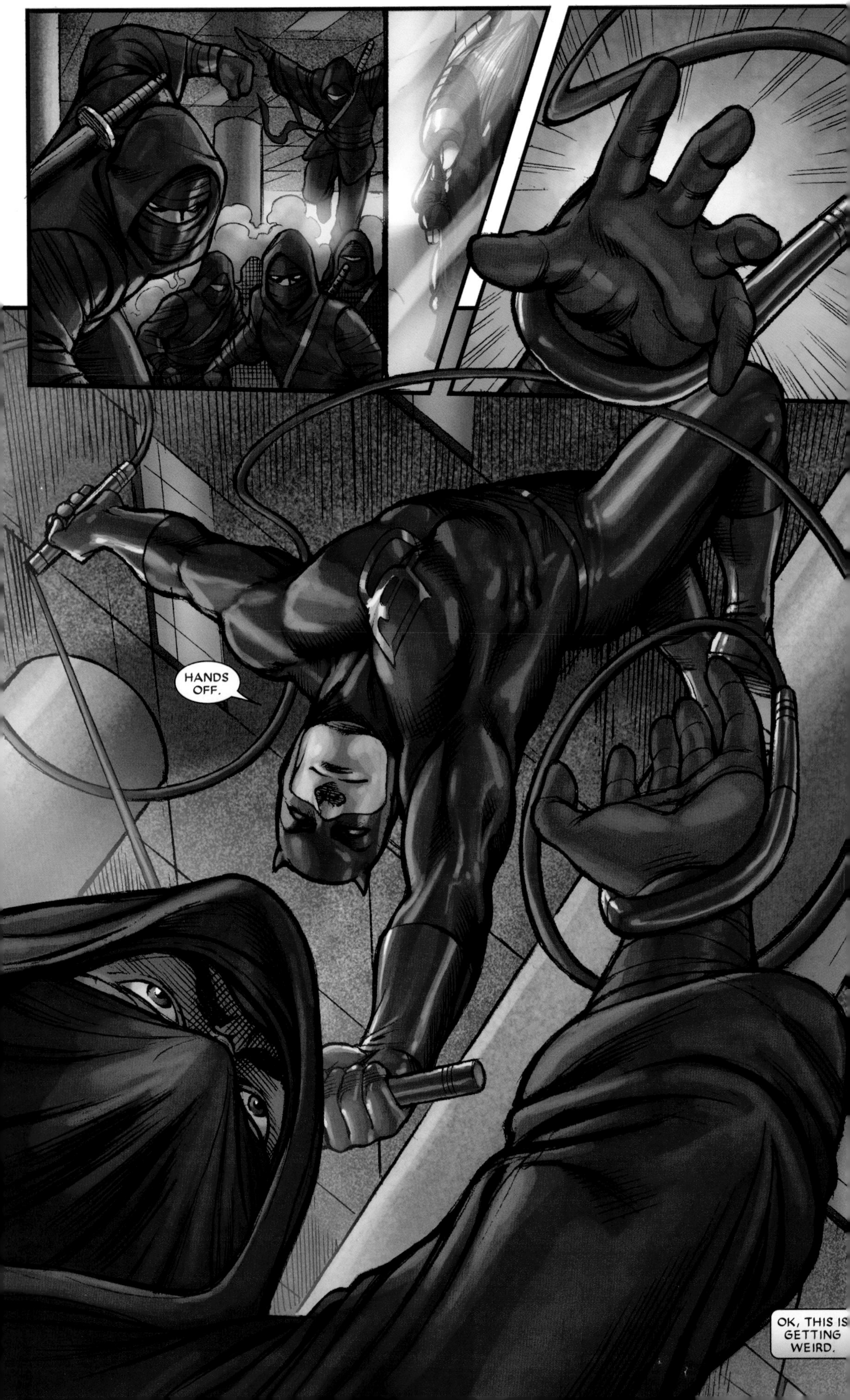
HANDS OFF.
OK, THIS IS GETTING WEIRD.

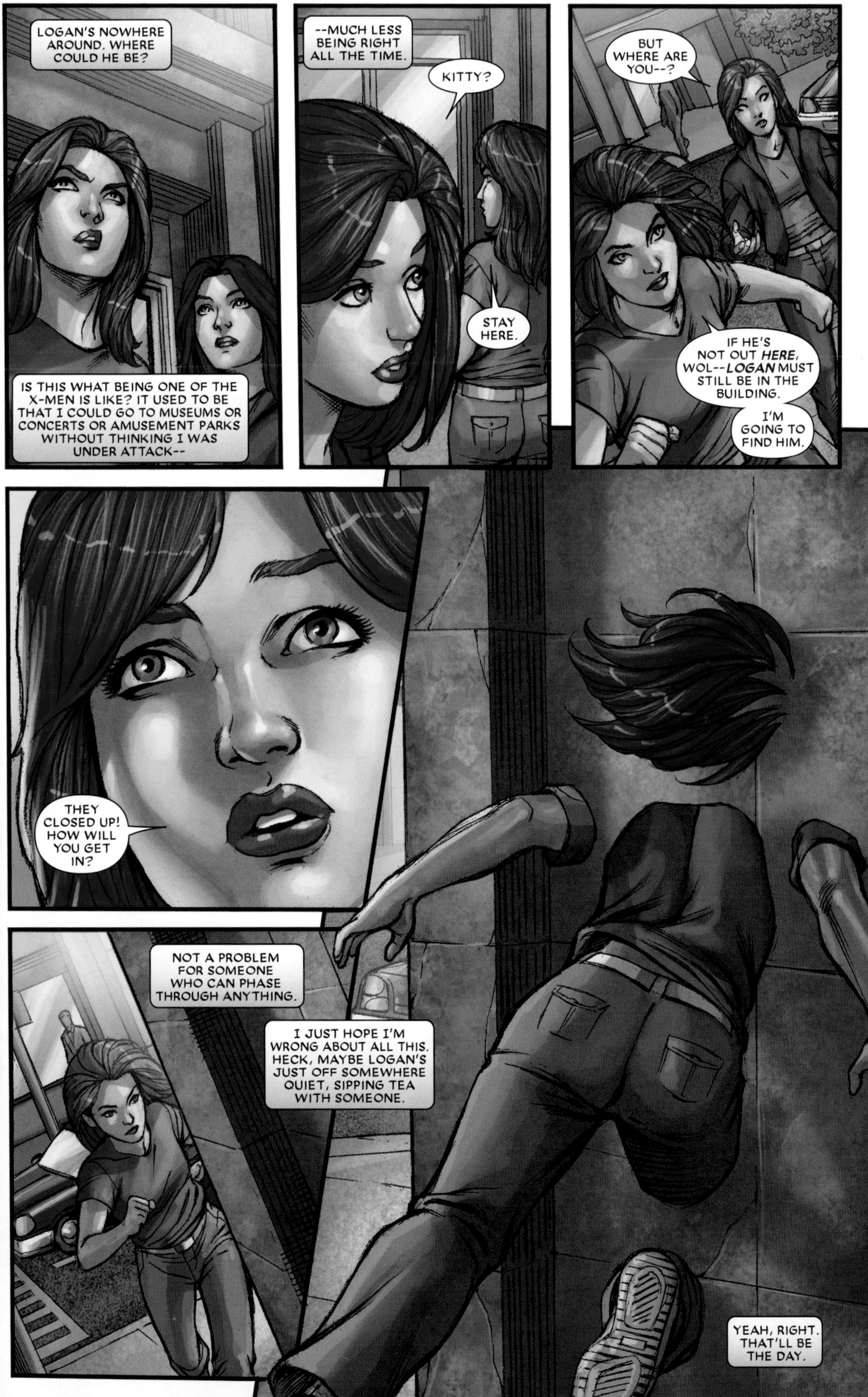
LOGAN'S NOWHERE AROUND. WHERE COULD HE BE?
IS THIS WHAT BEING ONE OF THE X-MEN IS LIKE? IT USED TO BE THAT I COULD GO TO MUSEUMS OR CONCERTS OR AMUSEMENT PARKS WITHOUT THINKING I WAS UNDER ATTACK--
--MUCH LESS BEING RIGHT ALL THE TIME.
KITTY?
STAY HERE.
BUT WHERE ARE YOU--?
IF HE'S NOT OUT *HERE*, WOL--*LOGAN* MUST STILL BE IN THE BUILDING.
I'M GOING TO FIND HIM.
THEY CLOSED UP! HOW WILL YOU GET IN?
NOT A PROBLEM FOR SOMEONE WHO CAN PHASE THROUGH ANYTHING.
I JUST HOPE I'M WRONG ABOUT ALL THIS. HECK, MAYBE LOGAN'S JUST OFF SOMEWHERE QUIET, SIPPING TEA WITH SOMEONE.
YEAH, RIGHT. THAT'LL BE THE DAY.

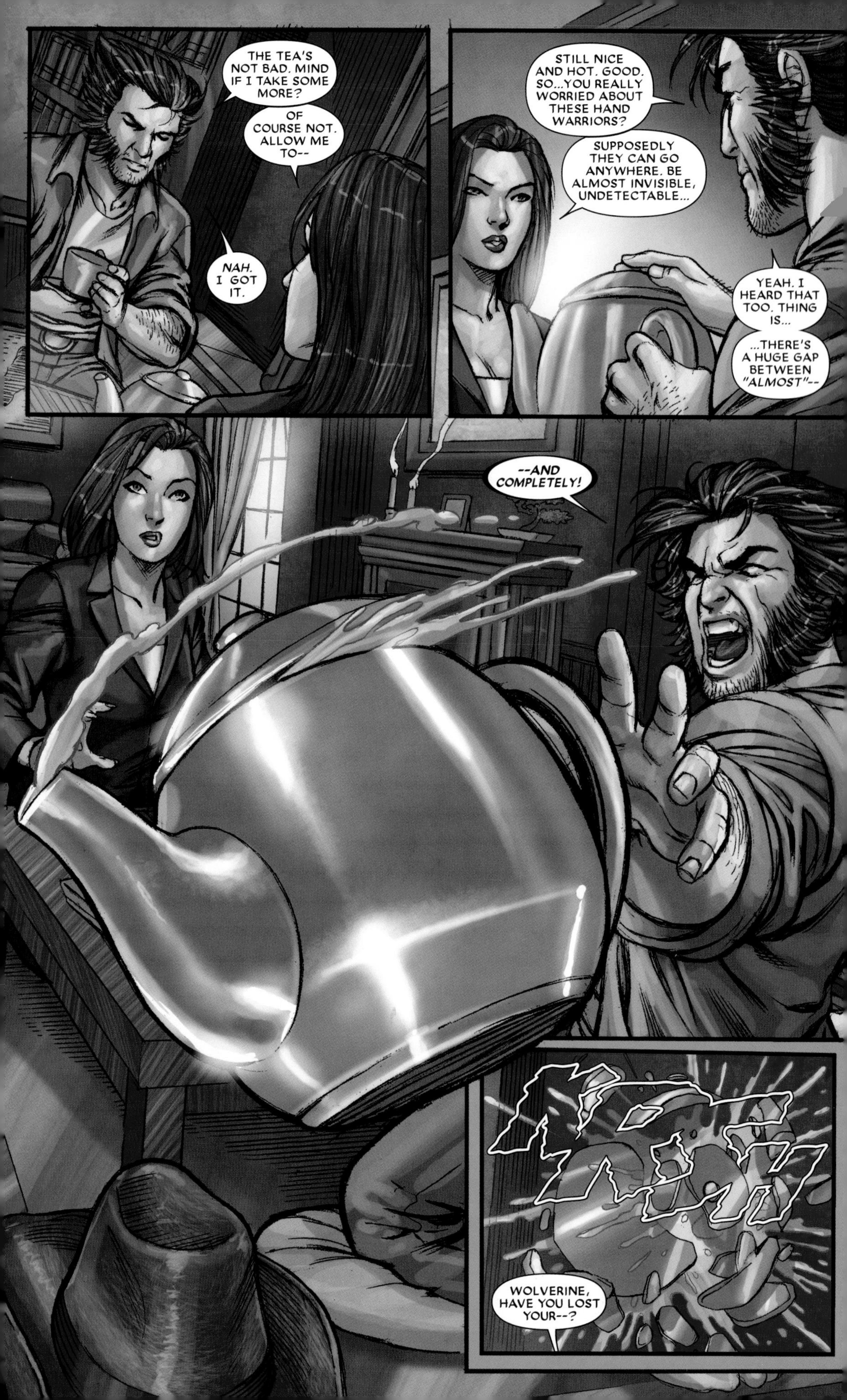
THE TEA'S NOT BAD. MIND IF I TAKE SOME MORE?
OF COURSE NOT. ALLOW ME TO--
NAH. I GOT IT.
STILL NICE AND HOT. GOOD. SO...YOU REALLY WORRIED ABOUT THESE HAND WARRIORS?
SUPPOSEDLY THEY CAN GO ANYWHERE. BE ALMOST INVISIBLE, UNDETECTABLE...
YEAH. I HEARD THAT TOO. THING IS...
...THERE'S A HUGE GAP BETWEEN "ALMOST"--
--AND COMPLETELY!
WOLVERINE, HAVE YOU LOST YOUR--?

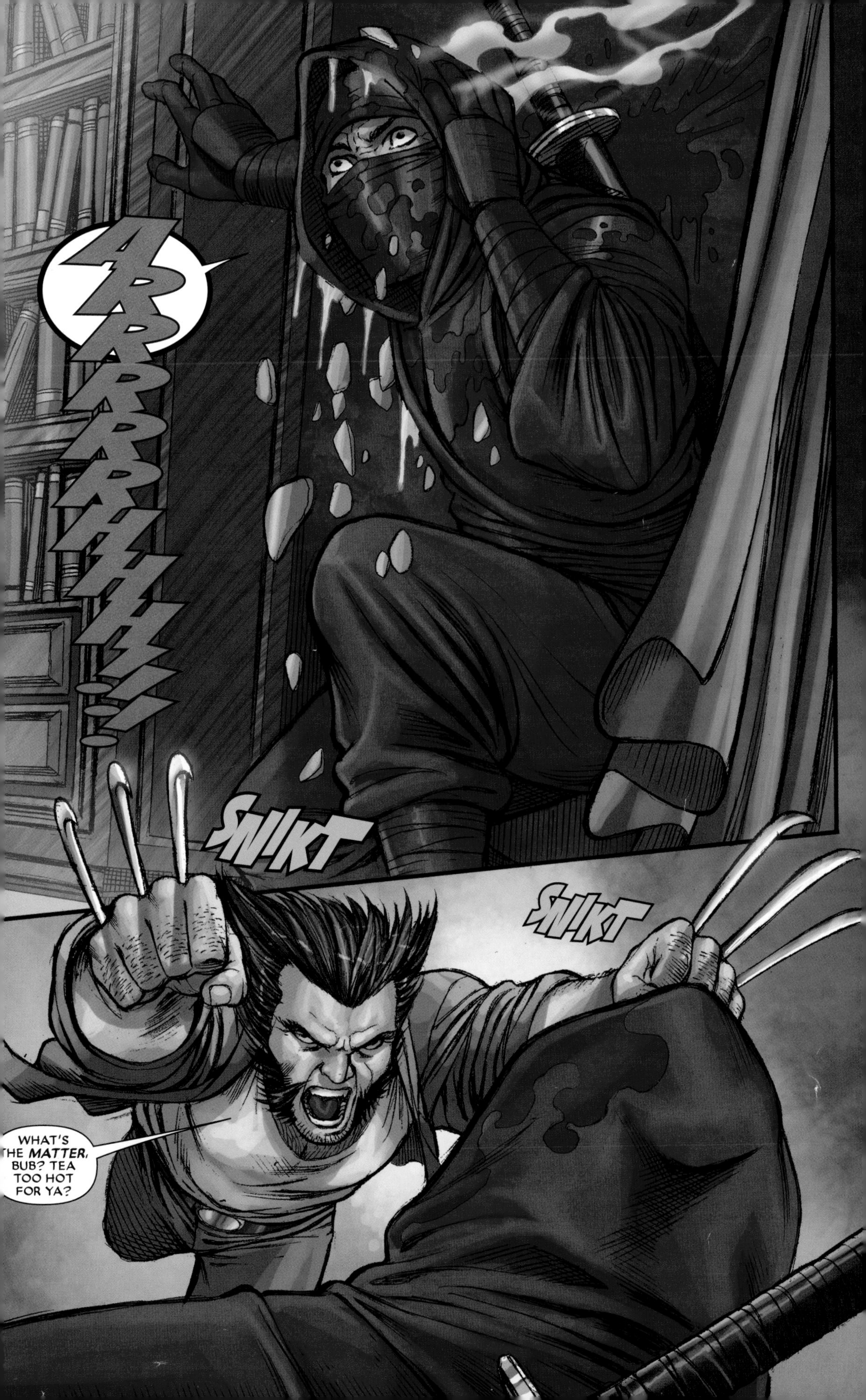

ARRRRRHHHH!!!
SNIKT
SNIKT
WHAT'S THE *MATTER*, BUB? TEA TOO HOT FOR YA?

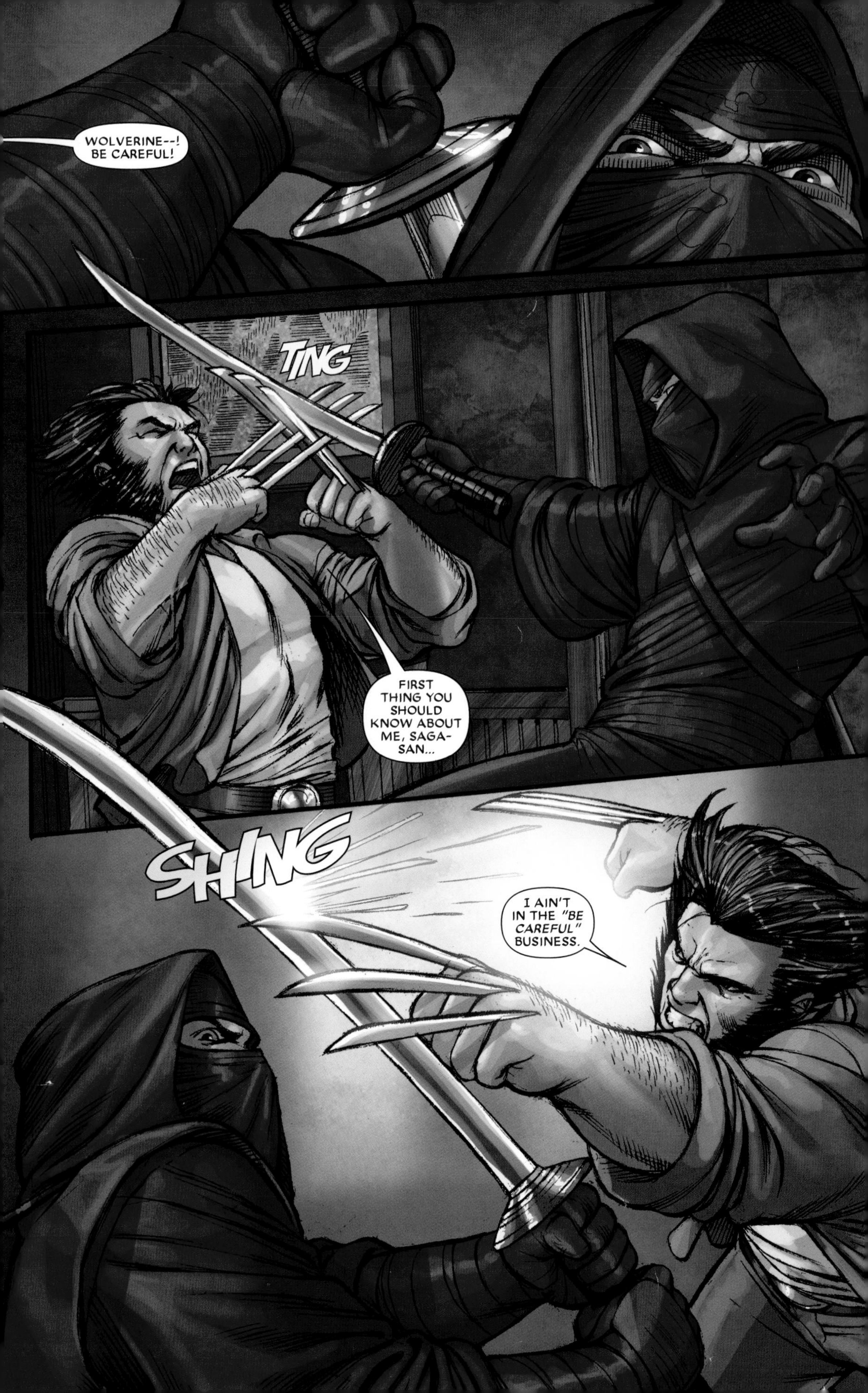
WOLVERINE--! BE CAREFUL!
TING
FIRST THING YOU SHOULD KNOW ABOUT ME, SAGA-SAN...
SHING
I AIN'T IN THE "BE CAREFUL" BUSINESS.

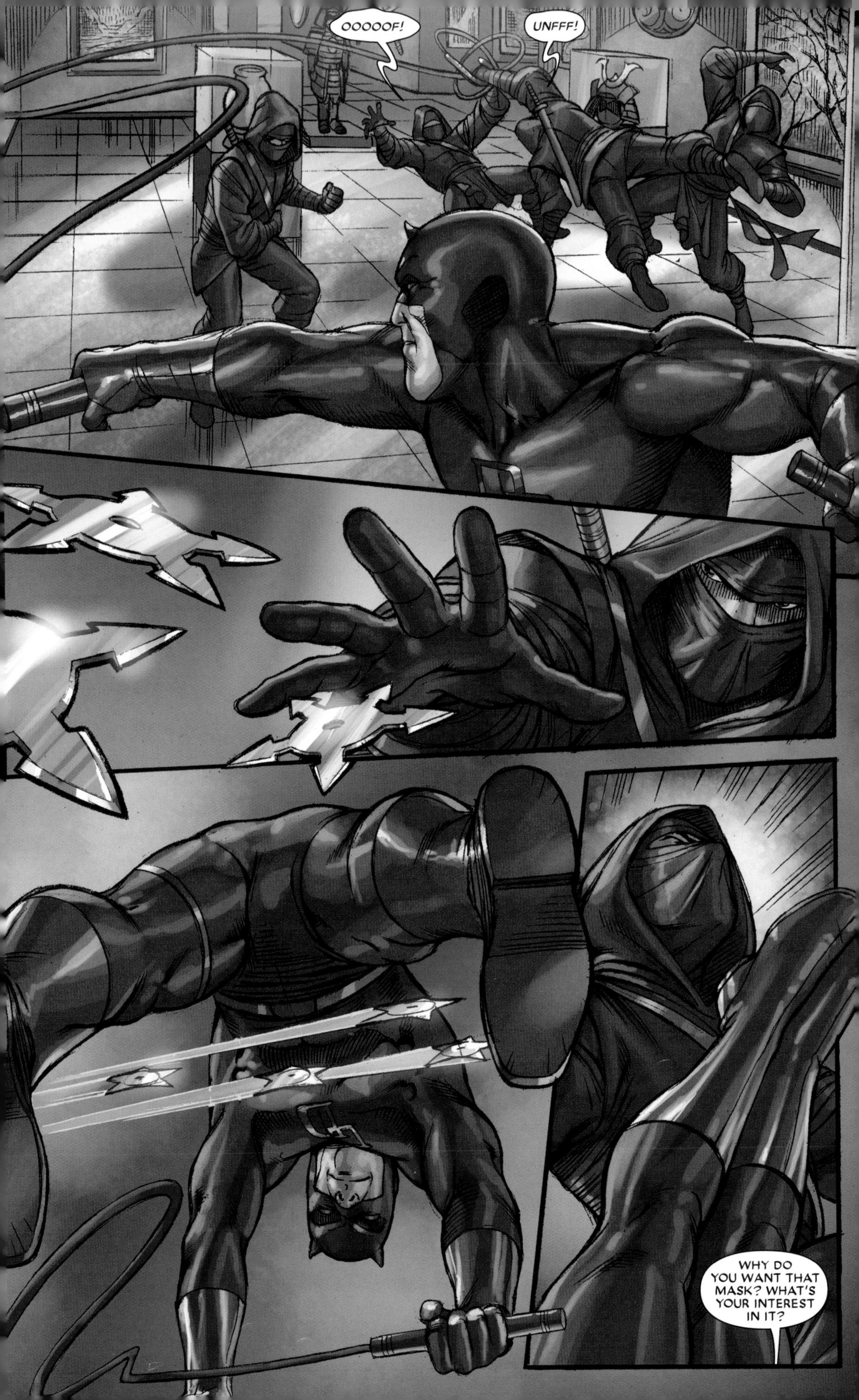
OOOOOF!
UNFFF!
WHY DO YOU WANT THAT MASK? WHAT'S YOUR INTEREST IN IT?

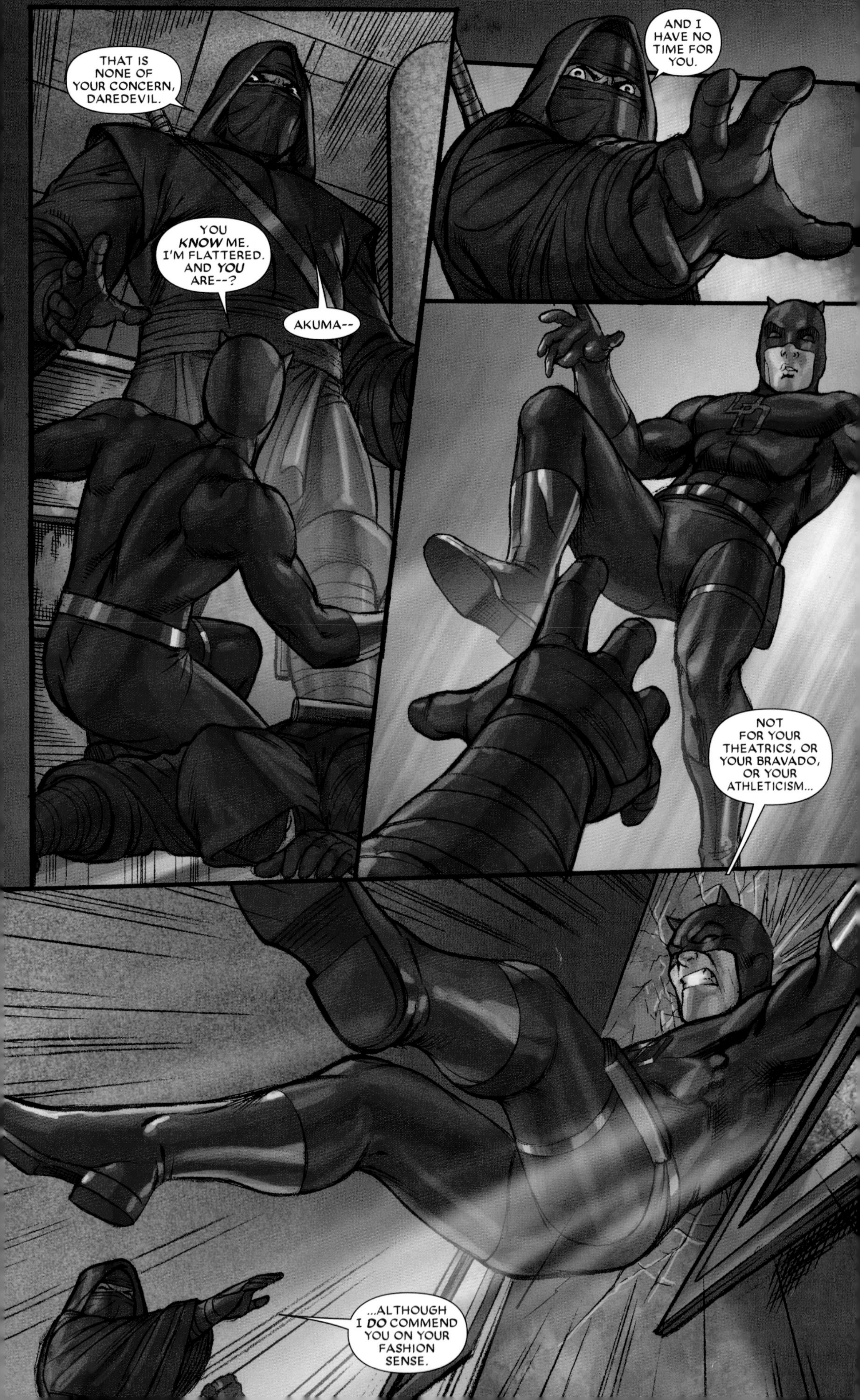
THAT IS NONE OF YOUR CONCERN, DAREDEVIL.
YOU *KNOW* ME. I'M FLATTERED. AND *YOU* ARE--?
AKUMA--
AND I HAVE NO TIME FOR YOU.
NOT FOR YOUR THEATRICS, OR YOUR BRAVADO, OR YOUR ATHLETICISM...
...ALTHOUGH I *DO* COMMEND YOU ON YOUR FASHION SENSE.

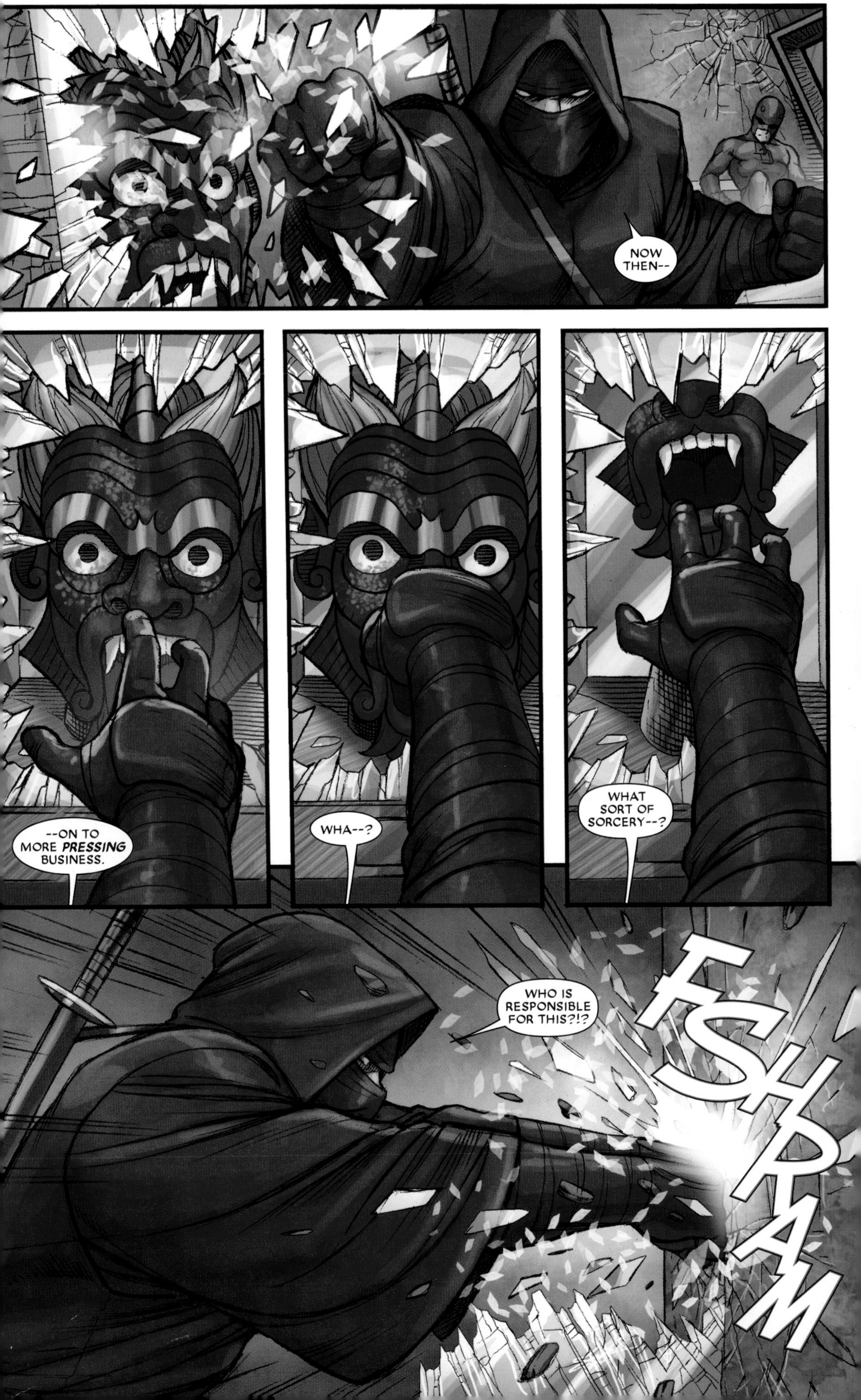
NOW THEN--
--ON TO MORE PRESSING BUSINESS.
WHA--?
WHAT SORT OF SORCERY--?
WHO IS RESPONSIBLE FOR THIS?!?
FSHRAM

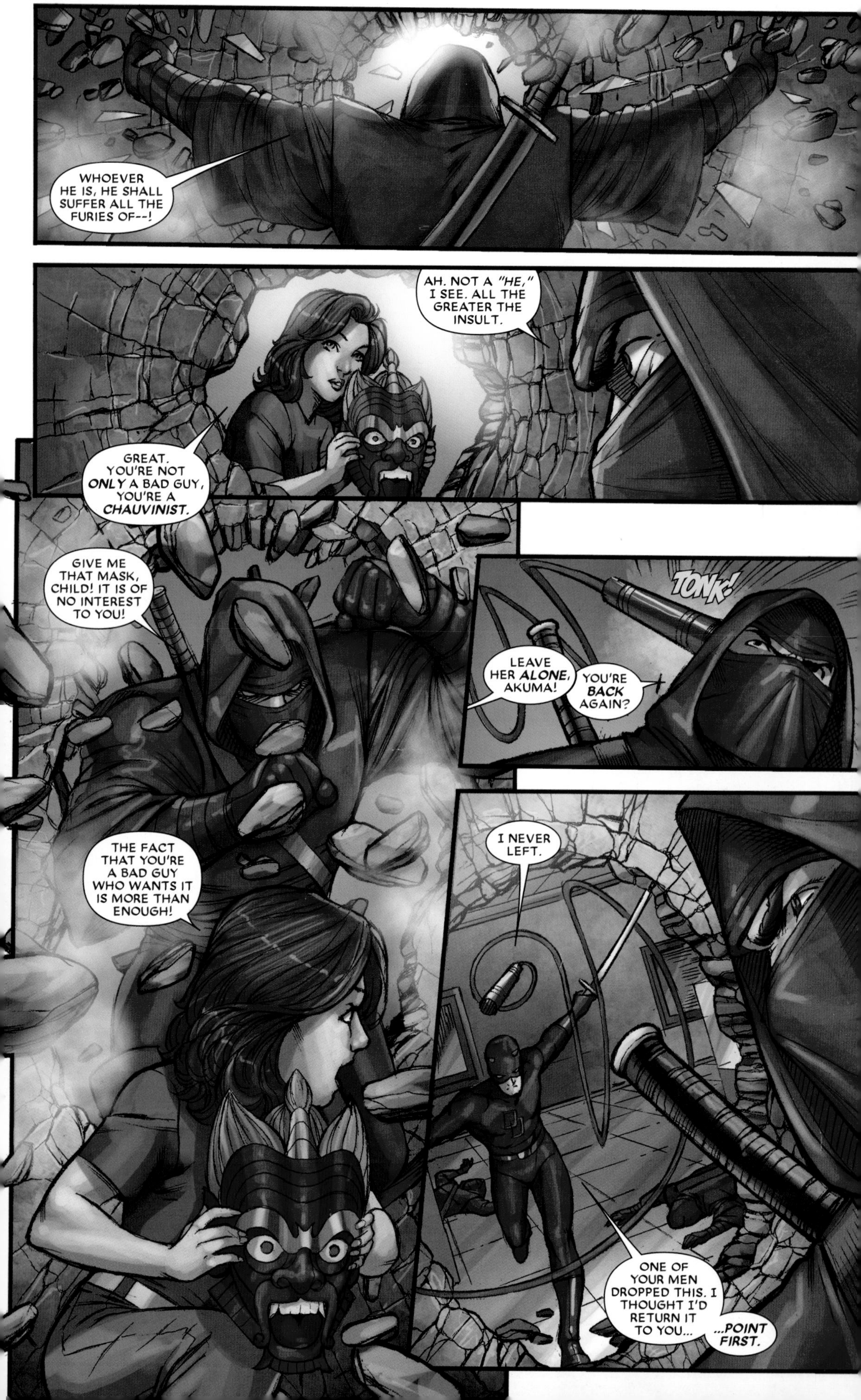
WHOEVER HE IS, HE SHALL SUFFER ALL THE FURIES OF--!
AH. NOT A "HE," I SEE. ALL THE GREATER THE INSULT.
GREAT. YOU'RE NOT ONLY A BAD GUY, YOU'RE A CHAUVINIST.
GIVE ME THAT MASK, CHILD! IT IS OF NO INTEREST TO YOU!
THE FACT THAT YOU'RE A BAD GUY WHO WANTS IT IS MORE THAN ENOUGH!
TONK!
LEAVE HER ALONE, AKUMA!
YOU'RE BACK AGAIN?
I NEVER LEFT.
ONE OF YOUR MEN DROPPED THIS. I THOUGHT I'D RETURN IT TO YOU...
...POINT FIRST.

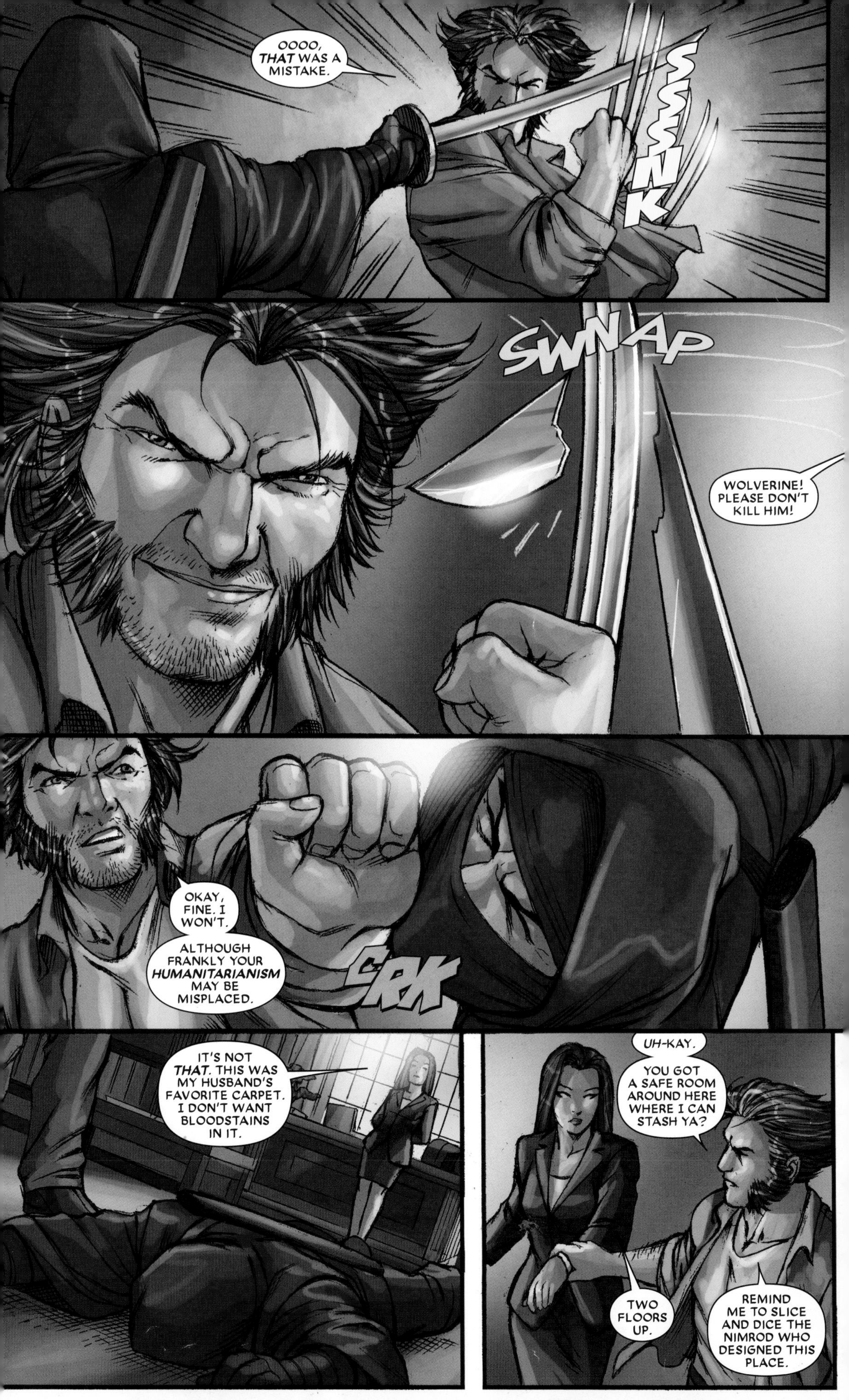
OOOO, THAT WAS A MISTAKE.
SSSNK
SWNAP
WOLVERINE! PLEASE DON'T KILL HIM!
OKAY, FINE. I WON'T.
ALTHOUGH FRANKLY YOUR HUMANITARIANISM MAY BE MISPLACED.
CRK
IT'S NOT THAT. THIS WAS MY HUSBAND'S FAVORITE CARPET. I DON'T WANT BLOODSTAINS IN IT.
UH-KAY.
YOU GOT A SAFE ROOM AROUND HERE WHERE I CAN STASH YA?
TWO FLOORS UP.
REMIND ME TO SLICE AND DICE THE NIMROD WHO DESIGNED THIS PLACE.

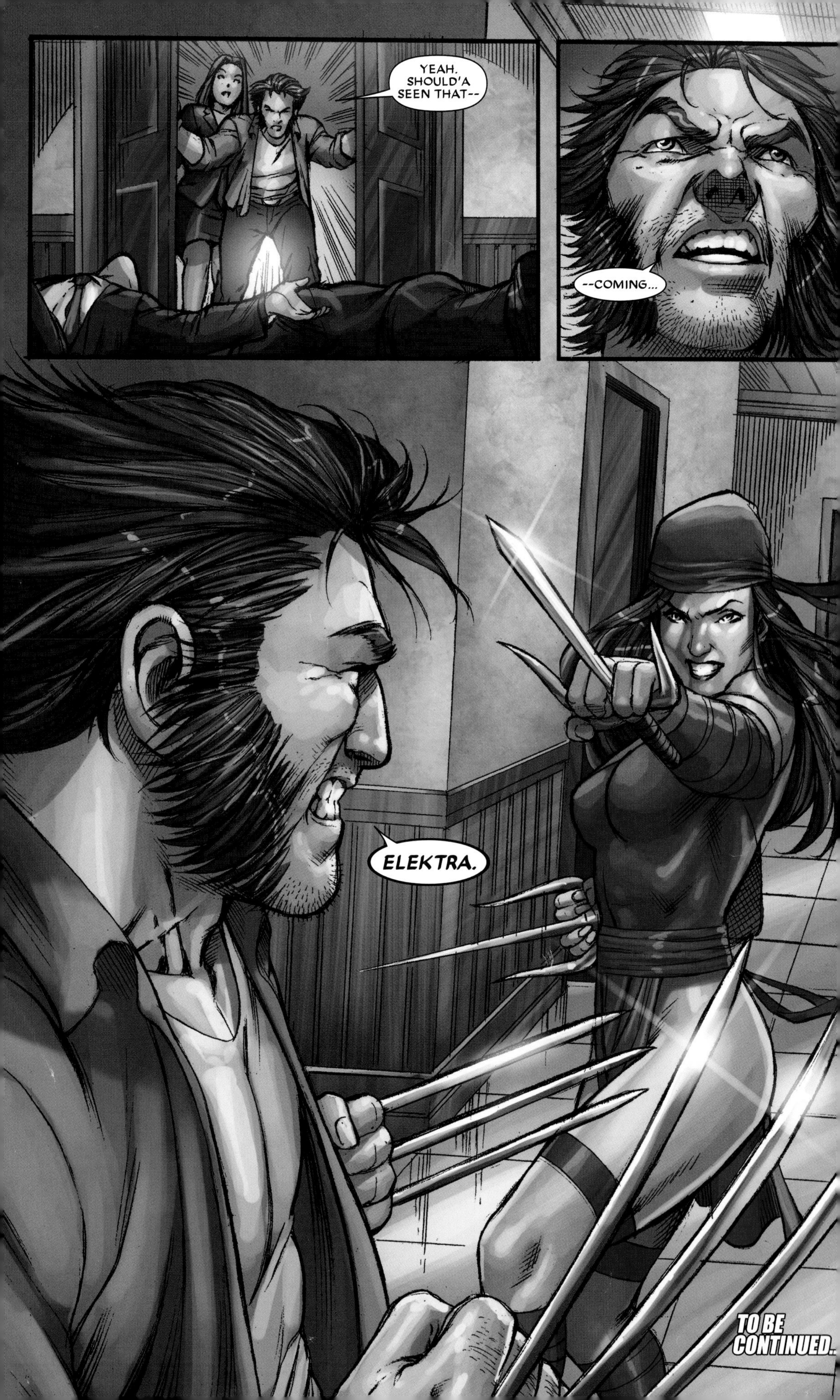

YEAH. SHOULD'A SEEN THAT--
--COMING...
ELEKTRA.
TO BE CONTINUED..